SNOWY RACE

APRIL JONES PRINCE

ILLUSTRATED BY CHRISTINE DAVENIER

MARGARET FERGUSON BOOKS
HOLIDAY HOUSE · NEW YORK

For my creative, devoted dad, who let me help at work, too.

Special thanks to the Shrewsbury, Massachusetts, Highway Department,
and to Margaret, Christine, and the Studio Goodwin Sturges crew.—A.J.P.

For my dear April and her wonderful family, with love.—C.D.

Margaret Ferguson Books
Text copyright © 2019 by April Jones Prince
Illustrations copyright © 2019 by Christine Davenier
All Rights Reserved
HOLIDAY HOUSE is registered in the U.S. Patent and Trademark Office.
Printed and bound in June 2019 at Toppan Leefung, DongGuan City, China.
The artwork was created with keacolor paper and ink (ecoline and colorex)
www.holidayhouse.com
First Edition
1 3 5 7 9 10 8 6 4 2

Library of Congress Cataloging-in-Publication Data

Names: Prince, April Jones, author. | Davenier, Christine, illustrator.
Title: Snowy race / April Jones Prince ; pictures by Christine Davenier.
Description: First edition. | New York : Holiday House, [2019] | "Margaret Ferguson Books." | Summary: "A girl and her
father set out in his snowplow to pick up someone special at the train station during a snow storm"— Provided by publisher.
Identifiers: LCCN 2018028294 | ISBN 9780823441419 (hardcover)
Subjects: | CYAC: Stories in rhyme. | Snow—Fiction. | Snowplows—Fiction.
Classification: LCC PZ8.3.P93 Sno 2019 | DDC [E]—dc23
LC record available at https://lccn.loc.gov/2018028294

Today's the day! She's on her way.

Flurry flurry.

Hurry hurry.

Growing flakes.

Quick hotcakes.

Whirl of snow.

Off we go.

I finally get to help!

Snowflakes start to tumble down.

Snowplow starts to head for town.

Wintry wind brings snowy showers.

Trusty motor hums with power.

Snow is blowing, falling fast.

Slip! Slide! What a blast!
Will we win this snowy race?

Frosty crystals chase and spin.

Snowplow shifts and tunnels in.

Beating, pounding.

Pushing, mounding.

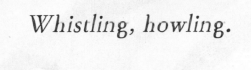

Whistling, howling.

Climbing, growling.
We plow with all our might!

Suddenly, a quiet spell.

Almost there! We whoop and yell.

Cloudy skies have more in store.

I scoot, then scramble, out the door.

Flurry flurry.

Hurry hurry.

One race done.

Another begun!